New School: Day One

Boston, Massachusetts

This is Rita.

She is from Mexico.
She lives in Texas now.

Rita is going to a new school. Today is her first day. She is **nervous**!

Rita looks at her **mother**.
"I am nervous," she says.
"I know," her mother says.
"You are **strong**. You can do it."

Rita gets to school. The school is very big. There are many classrooms. There are many hallways.

“Where do I go?” Rita thinks.

Rita goes to the office. “Hello,” she says. “I am Rita Flores. Where do I go?”

“Welcome, Rita!” the woman says. She looks. “You are in room 18.”

She gives Rita a paper and a **map**. “Have a good day!” she says.

Rita looks. The map shows many rooms. She has to find room 18. “OK,” she thinks. “First, I have to find the big hallway.”

Rita looks. “There it is!” she says. She is happy. “I did it!” she says.

Rita looks at the map. “Next, I have to find the gym,” she thinks.
Rita looks. “There it is!” she says. She is happy. “I did it!” she says.

Rita looks at the map. “Next, I have to find room 18,” she thinks.

Rita looks. “There it is!” she says. She is happy. “I did it!” she says.

Rita looks into the classroom. There are many students! They are talking. They are laughing. They are friends.

Rita is nervous. She thinks about her mother. "I am strong. I can do it," she thinks.

Rita walks into the room. She gives the teacher a paper. “My name is Rita Flores,” she says.

“Good morning, Rita,” the teacher says. “Please sit down.”

Rita finds a **desk**. She sits down. She puts her map by her **bag**.

Class begins. The teacher talks about school. He talks about classes. He asks questions.

Soon it is **lunchtime**. The students stand. They leave.

“I have to find the **cafeteria**,” Rita thinks. She looks for her map. “Oh no! The map!” she says. “Where is it?”

She looks. The map is not in her bag. It is not on her desk.

Rita walks out of the classroom. She looks. “There is the music room,” she says.

She walks. “There is the science room,” she says. “Where is the cafeteria?”

Rita walks. She looks around. Oh no! Rita is lost.

Rita is lost. She cannot find the cafeteria.

Rita is nervous. Then, she thinks. “I can do it!”

She sees a girl. “Hi,” she says. “Where is the cafeteria? It is my first day.”

The girl smiles. She has a paper. A map!

“I am Amira,” she says. “It is my first day, too! I am nervous. I do not know anyone.”

Rita smiles. “You know me. I am Rita! We can do it—together!”

The girls walk. They find the cafeteria.

Rita is happy. “I did it!” she thinks. “I have a friend.”

nervous

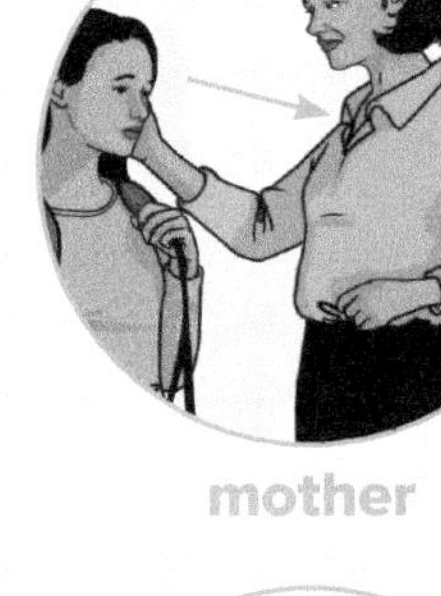

mother

strong

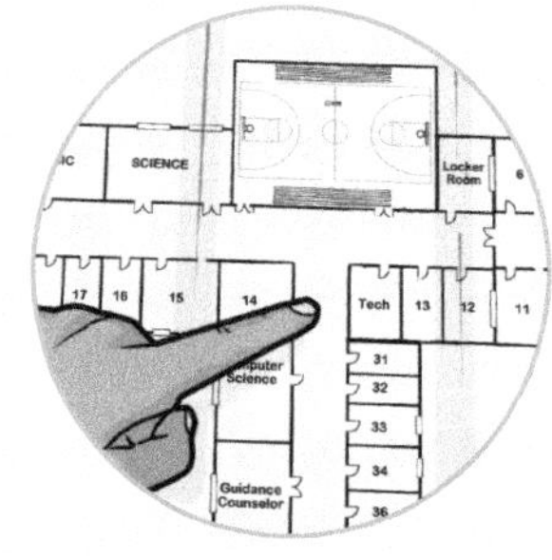

map

desk

bag

lunchtime

cafeteria